## Dear Parent:
## Your child's love of reac

D0188108

Every child learns to read in a different way and at his or her own speed. Some go back and forth between reading levels and read favorite books again and again. Others read through each level in order. You can help your young reader improve and become more confident by encouraging his or her own interests and abilities. From books your child reads with you to the first books he or she reads alone, there are I Can Read Books for every stage of reading:

### SHARED READING
Basic language, word repetition, and whimsical illustrations, ideal for sharing with your emergent reader

### BEGINNING READING
Short sentences, familiar words, and simple concepts for children eager to read on their own

### READING WITH HELP
Engaging stories, longer sentences, and language play for developing readers

### READING ALONE
Complex plots, challenging vocabulary, and high-interest topics for the independent reader

### ADVANCED READING
Short paragraphs, chapters, and exciting themes for the perfect bridge to chapter books

**I Can Read Books** have introduced children to the joy of reading since 1957. Featuring award-winning authors and illustrators and a fabulous cast of beloved characters, I Can Read Books set the standard for beginning readers.

A lifetime of discovery begins with the magical words **"I Can Read!"**

*Visit www.icanread.com for information*
*on enriching your child's reading experience.*

D0188103

HarperCollins®, 🏠®, and I Can Read Book® are trademarks of HarperCollins Publishers.

Bee Movie: Barry's Buzzy World  Bee Movie ™ & © 2007 DreamWorks Animation L.L.C. All rights reserved. Printed in the United States of America. No part of this book may be used or reproduced in any manner whatsoever without written permission except in the case of brief quotations embodied in critical articles and reviews. For information address HarperCollins Children's Books, a division of HarperCollins Publishers, 1350 Avenue of the Americas, New York, NY 10019.
www.icanread.com

Library of Congress catalog card number: 2007932785
ISBN 978-0-06-125169-6
Book design by Rick Farley

First Edition

❖

I Can Read!™

READING
2
WITH HELP

DREAMWORKS®
BEE MOVIE™

# Barry's Buzzy World

Adapted by Jennifer Frantz
Illustrations by Steven E. Gordon
and Kanila Tripp

HarperCollins*Publishers*

Barry Benson woke with a start.

It was a big day, and he couldn't wait.

"Barry," his mother yelled,

"your pancakes are ready!"

After a quick breakfast,

Barry raced through New Hive City.

The air buzzed with excitement.

It was graduation day for Barry

and a billion other bees.

"Barry!" called his best friend, Adam.

In a flash, graduation was over. Barry, Adam, and the other bees were rushed off to the Honex factory for a tour.

"We're here!" said Barry.
Barry and Adam were excited
about getting new jobs.

"Making honey has lots of steps," said the tour guide.

"There are many jobs,
and you can have any job
you choose."

Adam and Barry walked outside.

Suddenly, Barry saw the job for him.

"Check it out!" he said to Adam.

"Pollen jocks!"

Pollen jocks gathered pollen

from flowers.

They went on daring missions

outside the hive.

Barry wanted to go on daring missions, too!

There was just one problem.

Pollen jocks were big and tough.

And Barry wasn't.

A pollen jock named Buzz
decided to tease Barry.
"We're gonna hit a sunflower patch
six miles from here," Buzz said.
"Are you up for it?"

"Maybe I am," Barry said.

He didn't want Buzz to think

he was scared.

The next day Barry was getting ready to take off with the pollen jocks.

"Ready, hotshot?" said a pollen jock named Jackson.

"Yeah," Barry said. "Bring it on!"

Barry and the pollen jocks left
the hive.

They zoomed over the treetops.

There were kites, flowers,
and even people.

"Wow!" Barry said.

It was a whole new world,

with so many things to see.

The pollen jocks focused
on their mission.
They saw a bright yellow object
on the ground below.
"A flower!" Barry said.

Barry flew closer.

"Oh, no!" he cried.

This was not a flower.

It was a tennis ball,

and Barry was stuck to it!

"Ahhhhh!" yelled Barry

as the ball shot through the air.

Barry got free from the ball,

but he got sucked into a car.

"Yikes!" Barry cried

as he dodged swatting hands

and screaming people.

Then the sun roof opened. He escaped!

Safe outside,

Barry took a deep breath.

He looked around.

It was starting to rain.

And bees can't fly in the rain.

Barry found a dry place

to wait for the rain to end.

Finally, Barry headed home.

It had been a scary day,

but a fun day, too.

Barry couldn't wait

to tell Adam all about it.

That night, Barry fell asleep

with a smile on his face.

He'd had his first taste

of the great big world,

and it was sweeter than honey!

# More BEE MOVIE™ books for you to love:

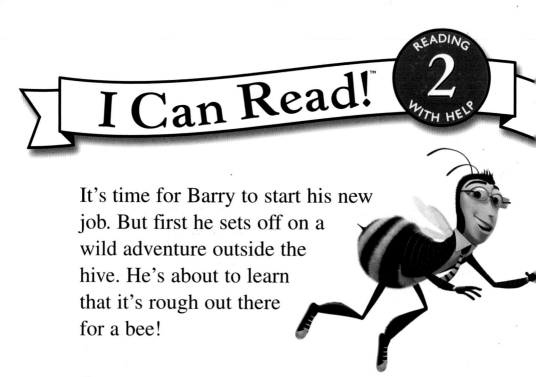

# I Can Read!

READING WITH HELP 2

It's time for Barry to start his new job. But first he sets off on a wild adventure outside the hive. He's about to learn that it's rough out there for a bee!

**My First** — Ideal for sharing with emergent readers

**1** — Simple sentences for eager new readers

**2** — High-interest stories for developing readers

**3** — Complex plots for confident readers

**4** — The perfect bridge to chapter books

**For more information about the I Can Read Book® series, see insid**

HarperTrophy®
An *Imprint* of HarperCollins*Publishers*
www.icanread.com

DREAMWORKS
ANIMATION SKG

Goodwill Thrift St
Books
Softcover Child
www goodwill

U
ISE
12-26
0230160110066602000

$1.00
Eac

9 7 0061-251696

## YOUR TICKET TO MORE *Curious George*®

Download dozens of fun activities to help reinforce simple math and science concepts. Enjoy hours of fun!

### GO TO: www.curiousgeorgebooks.com

Enter your secret password **LEARN**

## A FROG'S LIFE

Many animals change body shapes over the course of their life cycles. Frogs are one kind. Can you think of any others?

Here are the main stages of a frog's life, out of order. Number them one to four in the proper order.

FROG
(12–16 WEEKS)

EGGS
(BEFORE HATCHING)

TADPOLE WITH LEGS
(6–9 WEEKS)

TADPOLE
(BIRTH–4 WEEKS)

Here are some: mosquitoes, butterflies, ladybugs, silkworms, mealworms, ants, cicadas